Upside Down Wally

Written By Gene Brown

Illustrated by Anne Zimanski

To
Grandma Nat
and Grandpa Bill

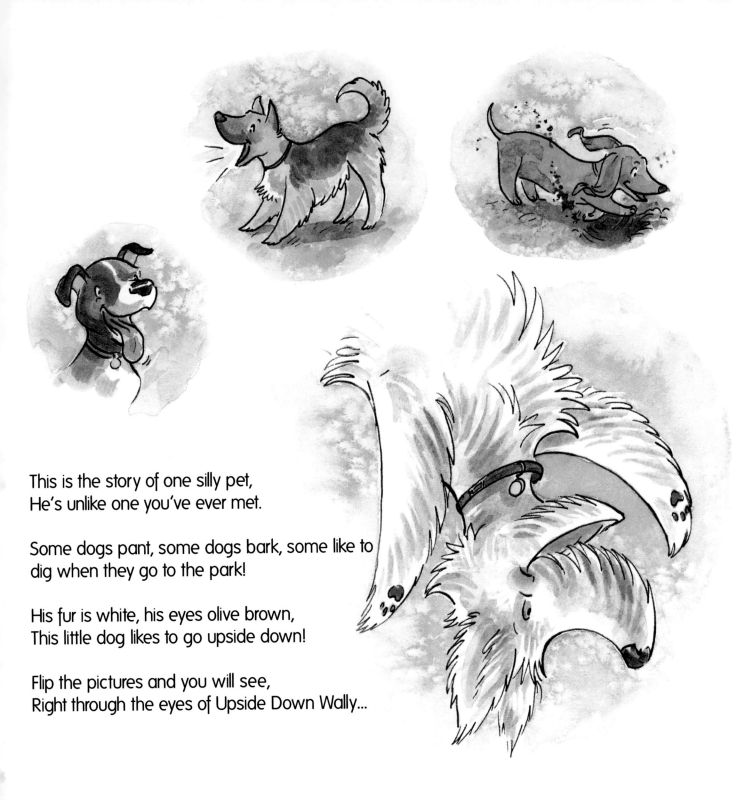

This is the story of one silly pet,
He's unlike one you've ever met.

Some dogs pant, some dogs bark, some like to
dig when they go to the park!

His fur is white, his eyes olive brown,
This little dog likes to go upside down!

Flip the pictures and you will see,
Right through the eyes of Upside Down Wally...

Here we are in the house,
It's so quiet you could hear a mouse.

But wait... do you hear the door?
Who's that down on the very first floor?

It's Grandpa and Grandma who just stepped in,
Grandma is holding a very large bin.

Here he comes! Sing along if you please,
He runs as fast as you can sneeze!

Trot, Jump, Flippidy-Dee!
Look through the eyes of Upside
Down Wally!

Can you see what he can see?

Here we are in the den,
There's sister Katie holding a pen.

She's writing something down and smiling hard,
Is that a cat behind her in our yard?

I wonder if she wants me to help her out,
I love when she scratches and pets my snout.

Here he comes! Sing along if you please,
He runs as fast as a swarm of bees!

Trot, Jump, Flippidy-Dee!
Look through the eyes of
Upside Down Wally!

Can you see what he can see?

Here we are in the kitchen,
Mom's baking something, could it be chicken?

Her fingers are blue with frosted glue,
I should not have chewed her pretty red shoe.

Something smells so very sweet,
I think I'll lick her fingers, it could be a treat!

Here he comes! Sing along if you please,
He runs as fast as you go on skis!

Trot, Jump, Flippidy-Dee!
Look through the eyes of
Upside Down Wally!

Can you see what he can see?

Here we are behind the house outside,
Dad is setting up the Slip 'N Slide.

Around the fence there are balls on strings,
Did you know that some ants have wings?

The balls are so colorful floating in the sky,
I think I can grab one if I try.

Here he comes! Sing along if you please,
He runs as fast as you can say cheese!

Trot, Jump, Flippidy-dee!
Look through the eyes of
Upside Down Wally!

Can you see what he can see?

I wish i knew what was going on,
Look! Around the house walk Norah, Deegan and Dawn.

With all of these people and family that i see,
What on Earth could this truly be?

Ding! Dong! Went the doorbell, HURRY!
Before the ice cream melts,
Out the back door walks someone else!

Their face is covered in yellows, whites and blues,
Look at the size of those checkered shoes!

Here he comes! Sing along if you please,
He runs as fast as a crisp fall breeze!

Trot, Jump, Flippidy-Dee!
Look through the eyes of
Upside Down Wally!

Can you see what he can see?

From this angle, it's now making sense,
Hey! Those are balloons on the picket fence.

There's Mom walking through leaves that haven't been raked,
In her arms is a giant blue cake.

That was a present Grandma had, not a bin,
Someone wipe the frosting from Grandpa's chin!

Sister Katie has joined us in the backyard,
She must have been signing a special card.

Now I get it! Someone's turning three,
It's a party for our brother Cody!

Let's say it together, loud and clear... Happy Birthday Cody,
from all of us here!!

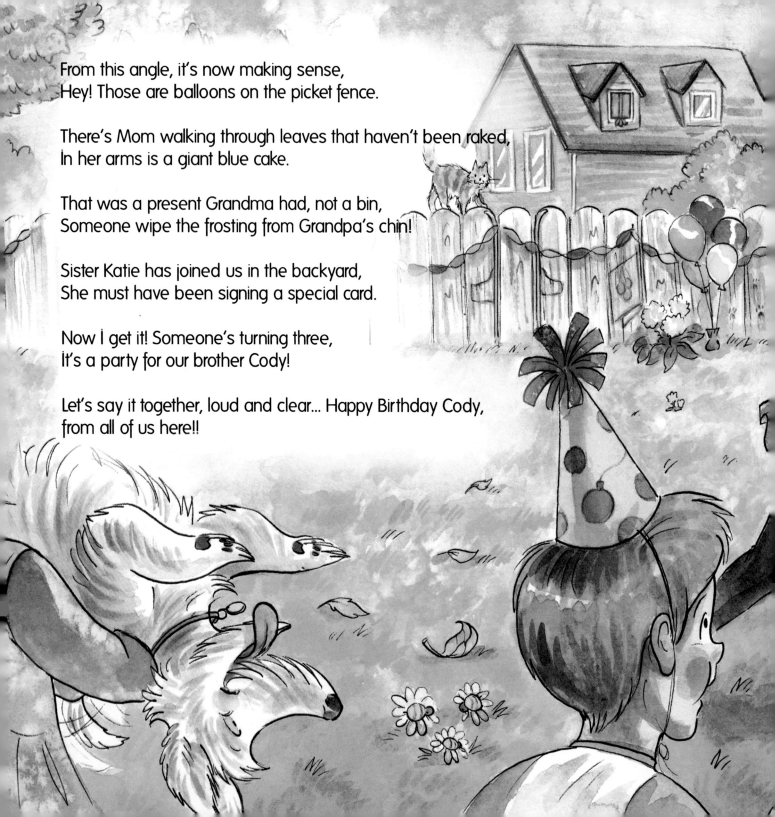

You've now heard the story of the word's silliest pet,
He's unlike one you've ever met.

When you're looking for something to do,
Try looking at things from a different view.

The world is a big and beautiful place,
When you see a sunset or stars in outer space.

The End

Just take it from me... Upside Down Wally!
Sometimes things aren't always what you see,

For a frown is a smile when you're upside down!
It's never scary when you see a clown,

The "Real" Upside Down Wally

"What you see in this world depends not only on what you look AT, but also, on where you look FROM..." -Unknown

A lesson idea for Teachers:

Looking for a fun activity to try in the classroom with your students? Have them draw a picture upside down! Students may not recognize the image they are portraying at first, but it will allow them to identify lines, shapes and their relations to each other - and this is when their true creativity will emerge. Artists do not always work logically; in fact, many great artists are always changing the way they look at art. It's amazing what you can do when you look at things from a *different view*.... Give it a try!

For more information on this concept and other drawing tips, visit the following web address:

www.allaboutdrawings.com/upside-down-drawing.html

About the Author:

Gene Brown was born and raised in Manchester, NH. He attended UMass Amherst where he graduated in 2007. While substitute teaching kindergarten in the months following college he was inspired to write *Tyler's Pumpkin Patch* after reading to one of his classes. *Upside Down Wally* is his second children's book to date.

He still lives in his hometown of Manchester where he works as a sales consultant for a medical device company. He enjoys working out, cooking, skiing in the winter, and being outside with friends and family in the summer. He's always working on making his dreams become a reality and like Wally, enjoys the beautiful aspects that life has to offer, from many different views.

About the Illustrator:

Anne Zimanski is a Michigan based artist, with a degree in Illustration earned from Kendall College of Art and Design. She knew from a young age that she wanted to be an artist, and always strived to constantly learn new styles and techniques.

Today, Anne has illustrated dozens of books and works on a wide range of design projects with people from around the world. When not working on art, she loves to spend time with family and friends, and relax on weekend trips to the Great Lakes to enjoy the beautiful sunsets over the Saginaw Bay.

Her work and contact information can be found at www.annezimanski.com.

Made in the USA
Middletown, DE
27 April 2017